THE ARABIAN NIGHTS
CHILDREN'S COLLECTION

Dados Internacionais de Catalogação na Publicação (CIP) de acordo com ISBD

J76z   Jones, Kellie
        Zobeida and the three qalandars / adaptado por Kellie Jones. – Jandira : W. Books, 2025.
        168 p. ; 12,8cm x 19,8cm. – (The Arabian nights)

        ISBN: 978-65-5294-179-4

        1. Literatura infantojuvenil. 2. Contos. 3. Contos de Fadas. 4. Literatura Infantil.
        5. Clássicos. 6. Mágica. 7. Histórias. I. Título. II. Série.

2025-598   CDD 028.5
                                            CDU 82-93

Elaborado por Vagner Rodolfo da Silva - CRB-8/9410
Índice para catálogo sistemático:
1. Literatura infantojuvenil 028.5
2. Literatura infantojuvenil 82-93

The Arabian Nights 10 Book Collection
Text © Sweet Cherry Publishing Limited, 2023
Inside illustrations © Sweet Cherry Publishing Limited, 2023
Cover illustrations © Sweet Cherry Publishing Limited, 2023

Text based on translations of the original folk tale,
adapted by Kellie Jones
Illustrations by Georgia Holland

© 2025 edition:
Ciranda Cultural Editora e Distribuidora Ltda.

1st edition in 2025
www.cirandacultural.com.br
No part of this publication may be reproduced, stored in a retrieval
system, or transmitted in any form or by any means, electronic,
mechanical, photocopying, recording, or otherwise, without written
permission of the publisher.
This book is a work of fiction. Names, characters, places, and incidents
are either the product of the author's imagination or are used fictitiously,
and any resemblance to actual persons, living or dead, business
establishments, events, or locales is entirely coincidental.

Zobeida
and the Three Qalandars

W. Books

Long ago, in the ancient lands of Arabia, there lived a brave woman called Scheherazade. When the country's sultan went mad, Scheherazade used her cleverness and creativity to save many lives – including her own. She did this over a thousand and one nights, by telling the sultan stories of adventure, danger and enchantment.

These are just some of them …

Zobeida
The third of five sisters

Safie
The fourth sister

Amina
The fifth sister

The Porter
A man hired by Amina to carry her shopping

The Three Qalandars
Storytellers

Caliph Harun al-Rashid
The ruler of Baghdad

Jamal
The caliph's grand-vizier

Mesrur
Chief of the caliph's guards

Chapter 1
The Story of the Porter and the Three Sisters

In the city of Baghdad, during the reign of Caliph Harun al-Rashid, a woman walked through a busy market. She was looking for a porter to carry her shopping, and she soon found one waiting to be hired.

'Pick up your basket and follow me,' she said in a sweet, clear voice.

caliph
A spiritual or religious leader in Islamic countries.

The porter looked up.

The woman wore a silken scarf around her head and shoulders that she also pulled across her face. All the porter could see were her eyes, which were very beautiful. So was the scarf itself. Even her shoes were embroidered with gold thread. In short: she looked and sounded wealthy.

With his basket on his head, the porter followed the woman through the market to a closed door. At her knock the door was opened by an old man. The man promptly vanished into the house and returned with a large, heavy jar, which the porter put in his basket.

The next place they stopped at was a fruit and flower shop. There the woman bought apples, oranges, peaches and many other fruits; then jasmine, lilies and many other flowers.

Next they went to the butcher's, the poulterer's and the grocer's, until at last the porter cried, 'If you had told me you were going to buy so much, I would have brought a camel!'

The woman laughed and told him to stop complaining – she was not finished yet. Next came the perfumer's, where scented water and candles were added to the porter's basket. They balanced unsteadily atop the meat wrapped in banana leaves, and the sugar cakes and the raisins and the shelled nuts ...

Finally, they came to a magnificent

poulterer
Someone who sells poultry birds, which are birds bred for eating.

house of white pillars. The ebony door was answered by a woman so beautiful that the porter almost dropped his basket.

'Come in, sister,' she addressed the first woman. 'Your porter looks like he is about to fall over.'

Through the grand ebony doors was an even grander courtyard full of carvings, and in its centre was a pool of water complete with a little boat. Beyond that was a seating area draped with net curtains. From these curtains emerged a third woman, even more lovely than the first two.

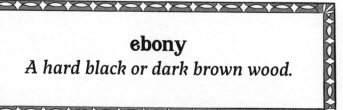

ebony
A hard black or dark brown wood.

'Do not just stand there,' she scolded her sisters. 'Help this poor man with his basket.'

Together the three women and the dazed porter lowered the heavy basket to the ground. The porter continued to stand and stare at the women even after he had been paid for his work.

'What are you waiting for?' asked the first woman, whose name was Amina.

'More money?' asked the second, whose name was Safie.

'Is two dinars not enough?' asked the third, whose name was Zobeida. She was the eldest.

'More than enough!' the porter hastened to assure them. 'Forgive me, I am only astonished at finding three such beautiful ladies all alone. Where are the men?'

'We need none,' replied Zobeida.

'Well,' said the porter, 'I for one would enjoy some company. Not to mention a rest and some food ...' the porter suggested.

The three sisters considered this, but were afraid of revealing their secrets in front of a stranger. Only when the porter promised never to say anything about them did they

---

dinar
The form of money used in ancient Arabia. Still used today in some countries.

agree to let him stay for dinner.

And what a feast it was! Safie brought the food and Amina the drink, while the porter made everyone laugh, even when not meaning to. It was a long time later – though not long enough for the porter – when Zobeida announced that it was time for their guest to leave.

'Let me stay until morning,' begged the porter. 'I will not find my way home in the dark. My eyes are not as good as they used to be. And my back still hurts from carrying–'

Amina was already laughing again. 'Oh, let him stay!'

'Yes,' agreed Safie, 'as a thank you for entertaining us so well.'

'Very well,' said Zobeida. 'But he must make a further promise that he will not ask questions about anything he sees.'

The porter happily agreed and the party continued even later into the night, until it was interrupted by an unexpected knock at the door. Safie went to answer and returned with surprising news. 'There are three qalandars outside!' Although it was more the fact that each of these holy beggar men was missing his left eye that had surprised her. They had just arrived in Baghdad and had come to the sisters' grand house to see if they might be allowed to stay in their stable.

'They are very polite,' Safie added, 'but they do look strange! Their heads, chins and eyebrows are completely shaven.'

qalandar
A wandering holy man. They do value possessions and often dress like beggars.

'With such an appearance,' said Amina, 'they would make our party even more amusing!'

Before she would allow the men inside, Zobeida insisted that they must read the plaque above the door, which read:

> He who speaks of things that do not concern him, shall hear of things that will not please him.

With this the qalandars were welcomed inside. After bowing deeply to their hostesses, their eyes fell upon the porter, whose shabby clothing matched their own. When they commented on this and wondered how he came to be there, the porter complained angrily: 'Did you not read the sign? Mind your own business!'

The qalandars apologised and the argument was swiftly smoothed over by the sisters so that the party could continue even more merrily than before. Soon their laughter was joined by the music of a harp, a lute and a tambourine. They were in the middle of singing loudly when *another* knock came at the door.

Earlier that evening, Caliph Harun al-Rashid had secretly left the palace with Jamal, his grand-vizier, and the chief of his guards, Mesrur. All three men were in disguise. As the ruler of Baghdad, this was the caliph's favourite way to walk about his city unnoticed and see what his people were doing. By the sound of music and laughter coming from a certain house, it was clear that some of them were having a party.

'Knock on the door,' he told Jamal. 'I wish to join in.'

---

grand-vizier
Someone like a modern-day prime minister. They did not just advise royal families in the old Turkish empire and in Islamic countries, they represented them and led the government. More powerful than a vizier.

The ebony door was opened by Safie.

'Madam,' Jamal said, bowing. 'We are three merchants who returned to our inn this evening to find the doors already closed for the night. We were wandering the streets until we happened to see your lights and hear your voices. With your permission, we thought that here would be a much better place to while away the hours until morning.'

Once again, Zobeida had the final say on whether the new visitors could stay. She told them gravely, 'You are welcome. But while you are here you

---

merchant
Someone who buys and sells goods.

must have eyes but no tongues; you must not ask the reason of anything you see, however strange it may appear, nor speak of what does not concern you.'

With this agreed, the porter, the three sisters, the three qalandars and the three merchants (who were not really merchants at all) sat down to eat. But the caliph was a curious man and collector of stories. He was burning with questions he could not ask. Who were these beautiful women? Why did the three qalandars all have the same eye missing?

Eventually Zobeida rose. 'Sisters,' she said, 'it is time.'

Immediately the food, drink and instruments were cleared away. The guests were moved to sit on benches against the walls, and two black dogs were led into the middle of the room on chains. Safie held out a whip.

The men stopped talking among themselves.

Zobeida sighed sadly as she gazed at the dogs and took the whip. 'I must do as instructed.'

To the confusion of their guests – and the growing curiosity of the caliph – the two dogs were beaten. Zobeida cried the whole time, but did not stop until her arm was weak. Then she kissed the poor dogs tenderly before they were taken back to where they had come from.

Amina and Safie tried to lighten the mood by singing and dancing. They were so enthusiastic that at the end Amina fell gasping on a pile of cushions, pulling at her clothes to cool herself. Her skin was covered in tiny scars.

The qalandars and the caliph-in-disguise whispered together, unheard by Zobeida and Safie, who were tending to their fainting sister.

'What does it all mean?' asked the caliph.

'We know no more than you,' said the qalandar to whom he had spoken.

'Do you not live here?' said the caliph.

'We arrived an hour or so before

you did,' answered all the qalandars together.

They turned to the porter to see if he could explain the mystery. The porter shrugged. 'I arrived a few hours before the qalandars.'

'We must ask them to explain their strange behaviour,' the caliph insisted.

Jamal reminded him of their promise not to speak of what did not concern them, but the caliph would not listen. He ordered the porter to ask on their behalf. When Zobeida looked back from caring for her sister, she saw that the men were talking earnestly together.

'What is the matter?' she asked.

'Madam,' answered the porter, 'these gentlemen beg you to explain why you would first whip the dogs and then cry over them. And also why the fainting lady is covered with scars.'

'Is it true, gentlemen,' asked Zobeida, 'that you have charged this man to ask these questions?'

'It is,' they all replied, except Jamal who was silent and disapproving.

Zobeida was furious. 'Is this our reward for the kindness we have shown you? Have you forgotten the one condition on which you were allowed to enter this house?'

Suddenly she clapped her hands three times. Seven guards appeared, each armed with a scimitar, which they held over the seven men, ready to cut off their heads at another signal from their mistress.

While the caliph regretted his curiosity, the porter complained comically that he should not have to die like the other men just for doing as they told him. Amina and Safie could not help laughing at him, even as their sister glared.

'Very well,' said Zobeida, 'then let *us* ask the questions. Who are

---

scimitar

A sword with a curved blade that was used in the Middle East.

you all? By your lack of manners, I assume you are men of low birth.'

The caliph saw this as his chance to reveal his true identity, but Jamal saw a chance for the caliph to learn a lesson for breaking his word and advised him not to. Meanwhile, Zobeida asked the three qalandars if they were all brothers, since they were all half blind.

'No, madam,' replied one, 'we are not blood relations at all, only brothers by our way of life.'

'And you,' she asked another, 'were you born with only one eye?'

'No, madam,' returned he. 'I lost it through a surprising adventure. After that I shaved my head and face and put on the clothes you see now.'

Zobeida put the same question to the other two qalandars and received the same answer.

'But,' added the third, 'we are not men of low birth.'

Zobeida told her guards to lower their swords. 'But stay close. Any man who lies about his history or his reason for being here will die.'

Seeing that he had only to tell the truth to be safe, the porter spoke quickly.

'Madam, you know already how I came here. Your sister found me this morning. She hired me to follow her to various shops, and when my basket was full, we returned to this house. That is my story.'

Zobeida nodded and said, 'You may go.'

'Oh, let me stay!' the porter cried. 'If the others have heard my story, I should hear theirs.' And he sat back down beside the sisters, while the three qalandars, the caliph, the grand-vizier and the captain of his guards remained in the middle of the room.

At this cue, the first qalandar began his story …

Chapter 2
The Story of the First Qalandar

To explain how I lost my left eye and became a qalandar, you must first know that I am the son of a sultan. My father's only brother was also a sultan, and reigned over the neighbouring country. He had a son the same age as myself.

As I grew up, I went to stay at my uncle's court every year. My cousin

---

sultan
A type of ruler or king in Islamic countries.

and I became very close. The last time I saw him he said, 'Cousin, you will never guess what I've been doing since your last visit! I would like to show you, but you must swear to do as I ask and not tell anyone.'

I foolishly agreed. He went away and returned with a woman of great beauty. He did not tell me her name and I did not ask. I assumed they were having a secret romance and she was someone not suitable for a prince.

'Cousin,' he said, 'we have no time to lose. Take this lady to the graveyard and wait for me there.'

By the light of the moon, I took

the lady to this strange meeting place. We had barely reached it when my cousin joined us. He carried a pickaxe, a container of water and a small bag of plaster.

He took us to a dome-shaped building like many others there. With the pickaxe he broke into the empty tomb inside and asked me to help him move the stones. As I had promised, I did as he asked. Under the dirt at our feet, a trapdoor was revealed. When I had helped him to open it, I saw a spiral staircase leading down into the darkness.

tomb
A room, usually underground, where bodies are buried.

My cousin sent the lady ahead with a candle.

'Thank you for your help, cousin. Please close the trapdoor after me. Then make a paste with the water and plaster and use it to seal the tomb as if it were never broken.'

'But how will you get back out?' I asked, already moving the door back into place.

My cousin smiled back at me through the closing gap. 'Do not worry about that,' he said. 'Goodbye, cousin.'

Puzzled, but not yet alarmed, I did such a good job of plastering the stones back into place that it was impossible to tell the new work from the old. I returned to the palace so tired that the events of the evening began to seem like a dream. In the morning, however, I woke to the cries, 'The prince is missing!' and realised that my cousin had not returned to the palace. I hurried back to the graveyard but could not find the same tomb, though I searched for days.

My uncle demanded to know where his son was, and I was forced to say that I did not know because of my promise of secrecy. Before I could be questioned further, I thought it best to return home.

At my father's palace I found the gate barred by a troop of guards waiting to surround me.

'What is the meaning of this?' I demanded.

I learned that in my absence there had been a rebellion, which led to the death of my father. His grand-vizier – a man sworn to serve him – was now on the throne. This vizier had hated me since I was a boy, when I shot out his eye by accident while bird hunting. I had apologised many times since then, but now he took his revenge by placing me under arrest and taking

rebellion
An armed fight or fighting against a government or leader.

my own eye. That is how I lost it.

Then he locked me in a box and ordered that I be taken into the desert and beheaded. But the men who had been told to take my head took pity on me instead.

'Leave this land,' they said, 'and never return. If you do, we will all die.'

Slowly, carefully, I made my way to my uncle. He was still grieving the disappearance of his son, but he joined me in grieving the death of my father, his brother. I made up my mind then to break my vow of secrecy. I told him about the tomb where I had last seen my cousin.

'My dear nephew,' he said, 'your story gives me hope. I knew my son was building something and I think I can find the tomb.'

We slipped alone to the graveyard. This time, with my uncle's help, it did not take long to find the tomb. We struggled to open the trapdoor because my cousin had sealed it from the other side. At the bottom of the staircase was a chamber, and in the chamber was a horrible sight. My cousin and his lady-love were dead. In their hands were bottles of poison.

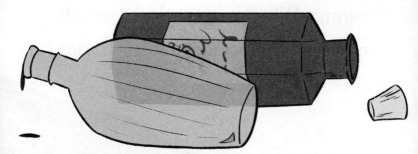

'I knew,' my uncle sighed, 'that my son was in love with this lady, whom it was impossible for him to marry. I tried to distract him with the most beautiful princesses, but he chose to die with her than live with any one of them.'

Again, we wept together.

When he had recovered, my uncle drew me to him. 'You are my son now, and I will be your father.'

On our way back to the palace, we heard the sound of drums and trumpets. A rising cloud of dust on the horizon told us that a great army was coming. When it drew close enough, my heart sank to see that the leader was my father's traitorous grand-vizier. He was coming to seize my uncle's lands too.

The city fell quickly, and my uncle soon after. I was now the rightful sultan of two peoples: those of my father and those of my uncle, yet I was forced to escape through a secret tunnel for their safety and mine.

And then to disguise myself so that I could travel unknown. That is why I shaved my head and face, and journeyed to Baghdad to see the famous and powerful caliph, Harun al-Rashid, and beg for his help and protection.

After many months, I arrived at sunset. I was deciding what to do next when I met another qalandar, just as new to the city as I was. It was not long before a third qalandar arrived, also a stranger to Baghdad. We wondered together for a while and fortune led us to your door, and we are forever grateful for the hospitality you have shown us.

'That, madam, is my story,' the first qalandar concluded, 'and my reason for being here.'

Satisfied that he was telling the truth, Zobeida nodded and said, 'You may go.'

Like the porter, however, the qalandar begged to stay and hear the stories of his two friends and of the three merchants.

Thus, the second qalandar began his story …

Chapter 3
The Story of the Second Qalandar

If you wish to know how I lost my left eye, I must tell you the story of my whole life.

I was only a baby when the sultan, my father, finding me unusually clever for my age, turned his thoughts to my education. I was taught reading, writing, mathematics, history, geography and science, and was soon better at all of them than my teachers. My intelligence became known by those as far away as India.

The Maharajah of India sent a messenger to my father with an invitation for me to visit his court. My father was keen to form a friendship with such a powerful ruler and accepted gladly. I set forth on horseback with the messenger and a small group of men, with a caravan of ten camels carrying gifts for the maharajah.

maharajah
An Indian ruler.

caravan
A band of people and animals travelling together, often formed for safety when crossing a remote area like a desert.

A month into our journey we were attacked by desert bandits. My men were either killed or scattered. I was injured but managed to flee.

Lost and alone, I journeyed until I reached a large city richly fed by streams, where spring flowers

bloomed in the wake of winter. By this time my horse was dead, my skin was sunburnt, my clothes were ragged and my shoes were long gone. I looked nothing like a prince.

I entered the city and stopped at a tailor's shop to ask where I was. The man saw my pitiful condition and begged me to sit down. In return I told him my story. He looked increasingly anxious.

'Beware,' he said at the end, 'of revealing who you are to anyone else. The prince who rules this land is your father's greatest enemy.

tailor
Someone who makes, repairs or alters clothing to make it fit.

He would like nothing better than to take you hostage.'

I thanked the tailor for his advice and hungrily ate the food he gave me. He even let me sleep in his house. When I was recovered from my journey, he asked, 'Do you have any skills you can use to make a living until you are able to return home?'

I replied that I was a poet, a writer, a mathematician, a historian, a geographer and a scientist.

The tailor sighed at my list of achievements. 'None of that will do you any good here. But you seem strong. Go into the forest to cut firewood which you can sell in the streets. I will give you an axe.'

With no other choice, I became a woodcutter. Very soon I was an expert and I was able to repay the tailor for his kindness. After a year I wondered further into the forest than I had ever gone before. I reached a beautiful green clearing where I began hacking at the roots of a great tree before I noticed a trapdoor beneath the earth. I cleared the mud and heaved the trapdoor to reveal a staircase.

I climbed down the staircase with my axe for protection, and I found myself in a palace set with marble walls and pillars of jasper, one of which was decorated with gold letters. Everywhere was brightly lit as if by open sky and sunlight, but brightest of all was the woman I saw there.

She looked as curious to see me as I was to see her, and even more

amazed. 'Are you human or genie?' she demanded to know.

'Human.'

'And what brings you to this place where I have been for ten years without seeing another human?'

'Fortune brought me here,' I answered. 'Good fortune after much bad.' Her beauty and sweetness inspired me to tell my story, after which she told me hers.

'I am the daughter of the King of the Black Isles,' she said. 'According to my father's wishes, I married a prince, but on my wedding day I was kidnapped by a genie and imprisoned here. Every ten days he visits with gifts of clothes, scarves and jewels. The rest of the time I am alone. I can call on him if I want to by touching the talisman at the entrance to my chamber, but I would rather it was you who kept me company.'

I stayed, and for the first time in over a year I felt like a prince. I bathed and feasted in splendour, with a companion more beautiful than any I could imagine. By the next day I was begging her to break her bonds to the genie and return

---

talisman
An object, often worn or carried, that is believed to protect the owner or have special powers.

with me to the world above.

'What you ask is impossible,'
she answered. 'Stay here with me
instead. It is not so bad. For nine
days out of ten I am my own master.
All you would have to do is take
yourself to the forest every tenth day
when the genie comes.'

But I was full of foolish bravery.

'Princess,' I replied, 'you fear the
genie, I do not. In fact, I shall break
his talisman into pieces!'

I had concluded that the pillar
with the gold lettering was the
talisman that kept her prisoner and
summoned the genie. The words

were some kind of spell. Before the princess could stop me, I strode towards the pillar and delivered a single kick. Immediately the palace shook and grew dark as night.

'Princess! What is happening?'

'Run!' she cried. 'Run or he will kill you!'

I disappeared up the stairs just as the genie's voiced boomed behind me.

'Why have you summoned me?'

'It was an accident,' the princess replied. 'I stumbled against the pillar.'

'Liar!' cried the genie. 'Whose is that axe? Whose are those shoes?

You have had company!'

Too late I realised that my hands were empty and my feet were bare. Grass tickled them as I climbed out of the ground into the forest and closed the trapdoor behind me. Then, to my shame, I ran back to the tailor while the princess faced the genie's wrath.

The tailor had been worried when I did not return the night before, but I could not bring myself to tell him of my adventure. Instead, I went to my room until he came to tell me that an old man was downstairs with my axe and shoes. The other woodcutters had told him where I lived.

'He is not an old man!' I cried, just before the floor of my room split open and the genie erupted though it. He seized me and flew me back to the underground palace and the princess.

'Is this the one?' the genie demanded. But the princess would not betray me.

'I have never seen him before in my life.'

'If that is true then take this axe and cut off his head!'

'How can I kill an innocent man?'

'You!' The genie turned to me.

'Take this axe and cut off *her* head!'

'Why would I kill someone I do not know?' I protested.

'More likely neither of you will kill the one you *love*!'

'Love?' echoed the princess. 'Have you forgotten who I am? I am the daughter of the King of the Black Isles. I was to marry a prince before you dragged me here. What would I want with a common woodcutter?'

She apologised to me with her eyes as she spoke. I did the same as I replied, 'A common woodcutter? Madam, I am no such thing! I am the *best* woodcutter in these parts

– as you appear to be the rudest woman.' To the genie I added, 'I can see why you keep her underground.'

'Rude?' the princess gasped. 'How dare you!' And she grabbed for the axe, which the genie raised suddenly out of reach. He looked confused.

'You really do not know each other?'

'Nor do I wish to!' sniffed the princess, and she started to cry.

'Madam,' I said over her

tears. 'Madam!' I repeated as they increased in volume. 'I apologise for offending you. It is only that I am proud of my work, humble though it is. Let us forgive each other, as the good man forgave his envious neighbour.'

The princess stopped crying a little too quickly, but the genie did not seem to notice. 'I do not believe I know that story ...' she sniffed.

'Then perhaps your fine friend will allow me to tell it?'

At the genie's slow, suspicious nod, I began the story ...

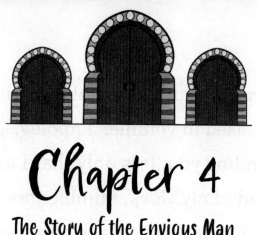

Chapter 4
The Story of the Envious Man

In a town neither big nor small, two men lived in houses side by side. One man was grateful and good, and everything he did he was successful at; the other man was jealous and mean, and cared only about harming his neighbour. So strong was the second man's envy and hatred, that the first man decided to move away. He sold his house and furniture and moved to the city. There he became a qalandar to live a quieter, holier life without possessions or wealth, so that no man would be envious of him. He became well known for his goodness and many other qalandar's went to stay and worship with him.

The good man's fame reached the ears of his old neighbour, whose spirit grew worse as the other's grew better. The envious man was still determined to ruin the good man's life so he went to visit him at his new home.

'I have something important to tell you,' he said, 'but it must not be overheard by anyone.'

While they were walking alone, the envious man pushed the good man down an empty well. The envious man then left, confident and happy that he had killed his old neighbour. What he did not know was that genies and spirits lived in the well. They caught the good man and lowered him gently to the ground, where he lay as if asleep – though he was wide awake really. The bottom of the well was pitch black, so he could only listen to the voices around him.

'Can you guess who this man is?' asked one.

'No,' replied several others.

And the first speaker answered, 'It is the man who gave up everything in order to end his neighbour's jealousy. But his goodness alone has been enough to make the envious man try to kill him. News of him has even reached the sultan, who will visit

tomorrow to ask him to pray for his daughter.'

'Why does the princess need this qalandar's prayers?'

'She is under the power of the genie Maimoum,' replied the first voice. 'If only this qalandar knew that all he has to do is find the black cat with the white tail tip that lives on his land. To cure the princess, he must take seven white hairs and burn them so that the princess can breathe the smoke. The evil spirit will leave her immediately.'

The genies and spirits stopped talking, but the good man did not forget what they had said. The next morning, when the sun was directly over the well and he could see his way, he climbed out. The other qalandars were glad to see him. Even the cat wound itself between his legs in welcome. The good man took this chance to pull seven hairs from the cat's tail and put them away until needed.

Soon enough, the sultan arrived. 'Noble sheikh,' he began, 'do you know why I am here?'

'Sire,' answered the qalandar, 'if I am not mistaken, you are here

---

sheikh
A leader of an Arab community.

because your daughter is possessed by a genie.'

'It is true,' replied the sultan. 'It is my hope that your prayers will save her.'

'If Your Highness will bring her here, I will see what I can do.'

The princess was brought at once. Her hands were tied to stop her hurting herself or others, and she glared as the qalandar placed a burning brazier near her head. The instant he placed the seven cat hairs on the coals, and the princess breathed in the smoke, they heard

brazier
A metal container for burning wood or coals. It is used for cooking or heating.

the pained cries of the genie being cast out forever.

The princess shook herself and blinked at her surroundings. 'Where am I? How did I get here?'

The sultan was delighted. He embraced his daughter and kissed the hand of the qalandar.

'I can think of no better way to thank you than to offer you my beloved daughter's hand in marriage,' he said. 'Do the two of you accept?'

The princess and the qalandar accepted. Shortly after the marriage, the sultan's grand-vizier died, and the qalandar became his new second-in-command. Then the sultan died, and the qalandar became the sultan.

One day the new sultan and his sultana were out walking among their people when he noticed the envious man in the crowd. He signalled to one of his men and said, 'Fetch me that man over there, but be careful not to frighten him.'

The envious man was brought forward and the sultan greeted him warmly.

'My friend, it is good to see you again. You shall be given a thousand pieces of gold, twenty camels bearing goods you can sell and an escort of soldiers to see you home safely.'

---

sultana
The wife, unmarried partner or close female relative of a sultan.

'But why?' gasped the envious man. 'I tried to kill you. I deserve punishment not reward.'

'This is neither,' said the sultan. 'This is forgiveness.'

Then he took his leave of the envious man, and went on his way.

'You see?' I asked the genie, at the end of the story. 'The good man knew that kindness is greater than anger, and that revenge would only hurt him as much as envy had hurt his neighbour. Not only did he forgive the man, he heaped riches upon him.'

'So I should do the same to you?' said the genie.

'The only riches I seek is to live,' I replied.

The genie raised an eyebrow. 'Is that all? Very well, I will let you live.'

The princess and I sighed in relief. Then the genie seized me and transported me to a mountaintop.

'I will let you live as an animal,' he added.

With a snap of his fingers, my nose retreated into my face. My back curled and my shoulders hunched until I was on all fours, looking down at the hairy hands of a monkey.

In a flash of smoke, the genie left me there. I had hardly needed my education as a woodcutter, but as a monkey I could not even speak words to call after him.

After learning to walk in my new body, I made my way down the mountain to an empty plain that led to the sea. I stayed there for a month until a ship came ashore, then I climbed aboard it. The sailors chased me, crying things like 'Kill it!' and 'Throw it overboard!' Finally, I climbed the legs of the captain and trembled on his shoulder until he took pity on me.

'This creature is under my protection,' he declared. The sailors left me alone after that.

We sailed for several weeks before casting anchor at the port of a large town. Many other, smaller boats came to trade with us, and one delivered a strange request from the sultan. He wanted each man aboard our ship to write on a piece of paper.

'You see,' the messenger explained, 'our grand-vizier recently died. He was famous for his handwriting and the sultan wants to find someone

port
A town or city with direct access to water, where ships can load and unload passengers and goods.

with a similar talent to replace him. So far no one had been good enough.'

One by one, the men wrote a few lines on a roll of paper. When they had finished, I darted forwards and snatched the paper for myself.

'Stop him!' someone cried.

'Leave him be,' said the captain. 'Who knows? Maybe he has good handwriting. I swear that monkey is smarter than my own son!'

'Maybe you should adopt him!' joked the men.

'If he can write I will!' returned the captain.

There was much laughter at this

idea, but it stopped when I took the pen.

Over the past weeks I had been well cared for, but I was anxious to become a man again. I wrote a poem in honour of the sultan, in the most beautiful calligraphy anyone there or anywhere had ever seen. The messenger took the roll back to the sultan, who took one look at my writing sample and ignored the others.

'Take the finest horse in my stables and the most magnificent robe you can find, give them to the one who wrote this poem and bring

calligraphy
An artistic style of handwriting, often very beautiful.

him to court so that everyone can see him.'

The messenger struggled not to laugh. 'Forgive me, Your Majesty, but the one who wrote this poem is a monkey.'

'A monkey!'

'Yes, sire.'

'Then bring me this monkey as fast as you can.'

I was brought to the palace on the finest horse (who seemed scared of me), wearing the most magnificent robe (which was too big for me), in front of crowd of people (who were shocked that a monkey should be

brought before the sultan at all).
When we stood before the throne,
I bowed three times to the sultan,
before stretching myself out fully
across the ground. People watching
were even more shocked now. How
could a monkey know the proper
way to pay respect to a sultan?

The sultan dismissed everyone
except his servants, and we entered
another room for dinner. The sultan
signalled that I should join him at
his table. I kissed the ground before
I took my seat, eating as carefully
and prettily as any human. Only the
power of speech was beyond me, but

I made signs that a pen should be brought to me. When it was, I wrote more words of praise for the sultan on a peach, then on a glass.

'This would be impressive for a man,' declared the sultan, 'let alone a monkey!'

After supper, a chess set was brought. I made sure to win enough games that the sultan was impressed and lose enough that he was not angry.

The sultan summoned his daughter to see me. At first she entered the room with her face uncovered, but the moment she saw me she drew her veil across it.

'Father, what can you be thinking of to summon me into the presence of a man like this?'

'A man?' replied the sultan in confusion. 'There is no one here save for the servants, myself and this monkey.'

'And that monkey is really a prince under a spell!'

When I signalled excitedly that this was true, the sultan asked his daughter, 'How do you know this?'

'The old lady who looked after me as a child knew enough magic to teach me how to recognise when someone has been enchanted and by whom.'

'Did she teach you how to break the enchantments?'

'She did.'

'Then do so and return this young man to his body so that I might make him my new grand-vizier.'

'As you wish,' replied the princess.

The princess fetched a knife with

words written on the blade. In the courtyard she traced a circle on the ground and wrote something inside it. Then she stood in the middle of the circle and repeated verses from the Quran until the air grew dark and the genie who had transformed me into a monkey appeared as a huge lion.

'You will pay the price for summoning me!' the lion roared.

The lion leapt at the princess, but she was nimble. She seized a hair from the lion's mane and with three words transformed it into a sword. She swung the sword so fiercely

the Quran
The holy book of Islam used in the Muslim religion.

that the genie was forced to become something else or risk being cut to pieces. In the lion's place there was now a scorpion. The scorpion advanced, deadly stinger raised, but the princess transformed into a snake. The two battled on, until the

genie again retreated into a different form. This time he became an eagle and tried to fly away, but the princess became an even stronger eagle and followed him out of our sight.

We waited anxiously to find out who would be the winner. It was hardly proper, but I was perched on the sultan's shoulder now, and we clutched at each other in fright as the floor split open and spat forth a cat with black and white fur stood all on end in fury. It hissed at the wolf who came after it out of the ground, only now we did not know who was who.

'I pray my daughter is the wolf!' cried the sultan.

But just as it looked like the wolf was about to catch it, the cat became a worm and burrowed into a pomegranate that had fallen from a nearby tree. The pomegranate swelled to the size of a pumpkin, then hovered to the height of the surrounding courtyard walls. It then fell from this height and smashed across the floor.

The wolf became a rooster and began pecking at the pomegranate seeds.

'It is eating it!' the sultan gasped. I, of course, could say nothing, though my fate depended on the outcome of this fight.

When all but one of the seeds was eaten, the rooster moved to eat the final one. Before it could, however, the seed rolled into a stream and became a fish. The rooster became a bigger fish and went in after it. The genie burst out of the water breathing fire, which could not harm the princess whose body was now made up of burning coals. They fought until the courtyard was full of smoke and the palace was at risk of burning to the ground. An ember struck my left eye. The sultan's beard was badly singed.

Finally, we heard the princess cry, 'I have won!'

The genie was ashes at her feet.

The servant brought the princess

a glass of water, but rather than drink it she dashed it in my face. She said, 'If you are only a monkey by magic, return now to the form you had before.' In an instant I stood before her in my old body, minus one eye.

'Daughter!' exclaimed the sultan. 'You have done well! You must marry the prince as your reward, for I see now that you are as clever as he is!'

'Then am I not clever enough to decide my own reward?'

'Why, yes,' said the sultan. 'I suppose you are …'

'Well, I choose never to marry but to be your new grand-vizier instead.'

The sultan agreed and with her new power, the princess-turned-grand-vizier asked me to leave.

'Even if you are not cleverer than I am,' she said, 'your handwriting is better! A woman grand-vizier will have enough troubles without such competition.'

'I owe you my life,' I told her. 'Of course I will leave, and with thanks for your help.'

Before I left the palace, I shaved my head and face and put on the clothes of a qalandar. Not knowing what else to do, I came to Baghdad to see the Commander of the Faithful, Caliph Harun al-Rashid.

'That, madam, is my story,' the second qalandar concluded, 'and my reason for being here.'

Satisfied that he was telling the truth, Zobeida nodded and said, 'You may go.'

But once again, the second qalandar chose to stay. He took his seat with the sisters, the porter and the first qalandar, so that the third qalandar could begin his story …

Chapter 5
The Story of the Third Qalandar

My name is Agib, and I am the son of a sultan called Cassib, who reigned over a large kingdom. The capital of that kingdom was one of the finest ports in the world.

When I inherited my father's throne, my first duty was to travel the land to gain the love and loyalty of my people. This meant visiting many islands, which gave me such a taste for sailing that I soon wanted to explore further. At my command, a fleet of ships were built and I set out to discover new lands.

For forty days we sailed with the wind in our favour, but on the forty-first a terrible storm arose. For the next two days, we were blown this way and that. 'Allah be praised!' I said when the wind dropped and the seas were calm again. But now the captain had no idea where we were. He sent a sailor to climb the mast and look for land.

'I see nothing but sea and sky

Allah
The Arabic word for God, used in the Muslim religion.

ahead of us,' the sailor reported back, 'and darkness beyond.'

At his words, the captain's face turned white below his turban.

'We have drifted far off course, sire,' he told me. 'That darkness is the Black Mountain. By tomorrow we will reach it. The mountain is made of a material known as adamant. It attracts all other metals towards it – including the iron and nails that hold our ship together. See how they cling to the mountainside, making it black? Without iron and nails in our ship, we will sink.

'At the top of the mountain is a

brass dome with a statue of a brass horse and rider on top. The rider's lead breastplate is enchanted. It is said that as long as that statue stands, ships and their sailors will continue to die at the foot of the mountain.'

The captain was crying now, and the crew began to prepare for their deaths.

At noon the next day, we reached the Black Mountain. The closer we got the stronger the magnetic pull became and the faster we moved. We watched as iron and nails were torn from the ships ahead of us and dashed against the mountain with a deafening sound. The ships themselves began to fall apart and sink. The crews sank with them.

When it was our turn, I managed to grasp a floating plank, and was driven ashore by the wind. I was the only survivor.

I say 'shore', but there was hardly any flat ground to stand on, only the narrowest of steps leading up the mountainside. The slightest of breezes could have blown me back into the sea, or impaled me on the jagged slopes, but I reached the top unharmed.

'Allah be praised,' I sighed gratefully.

There was the brass dome, exactly

as the captain had described, but I was too tired to do anything more than use it for shelter and sleep. In my dreams an old man appeared and said, 'Listen, Agib! When you wake you must dig the ground until you find a brass bow with three lead arrows. Shoot these at the statue and the rider will tumble into the sea, but the horse will tumble to the ground. Then you must bury the horse where you dug up the bow and arrows. When this is done, the sea will rise and bring you a boat. As long as you do not say Allah's name, you will be saved.'

I woke and followed this advice.
I found the bow and arrows, shot the
rider so that he fell into the sea and
his brass horse fell into the hole I
had dug. The sea immediately began
to rise. I had barely enough time to
bury the horse before a metal man

in a boat drew level with me as the mountain was swallowed by the sea.

The metal man rowed for nine days straight, after which land appeared on the horizon. I was so overcome with joy at the sight that I forgot what the old man had told me. I cried out, 'Allah be praised!'

The instant the words left my mouth, the boat sank and the man disappeared. All that day and night I took turns swimming and floating, aiming for the island nearest to me. When I was at the end of my strength and about to give up hope of making it, the wind picked up and a huge wave delivered me the rest of the way.

There seemed to be no one but me on this new island, which was covered in fruit trees and watered by streams. It was a long way from the mainland. Before this could discourage me, however, I saw a ship heading my way. I hid in the branches of a tree while the sailors came ashore carrying spades. In the middle of the island they stopped and started digging. I watched as they uncovered what appeared to be a trapdoor, then went back to the ship to unload food, furniture

and clothing, and carry them underground. Lastly, they brought an old man and a boy of about fifteen years old, and they too went below. When the sailors and the old man came back out, the boy did not. I watched, amazed, as they covered the trapdoor back over with dirt and set sail without him.

Once their ship was too far off to see me, I came down from my tree. I went to the place where the boy was buried. Then I dug up the earth, pulled up the trapdoor and uncovered a set of stone steps. They led me to a chamber richly furnished and lit by candles. On a pile of cushions sat the boy.

'Do not be alarmed,' I reassured him. 'I am here to help not harm you. Why have they left you here?'

'My father is a rich merchant. He always dreamt of having a son to inherit his wealth and when I was finally born, he consulted all the wise men in the land to learn my future. They all said the same thing: I would live happily until my fifteenth year, when a terrible danger awaited me. Only if I escaped this danger would I live to be an old man. Otherwise I would die at the hand of Agib, son of Cassib, fifty days after he shot the brass horseman from the top of the Black Mountain.'

I hid my surprise at hearing my own name from the mouth of this unknown boy.

'Nine days ago,' he continued, 'we heard that the brass horseman had fallen into the sea. My father decided that I must go into hiding until the danger of Prince Agib finding me has passed. And what better place to hide than underground in the middle of a deserted island? No one is likely to find me here!'

I nodded my agreement and decided not to tell him my real name. I had no intention of killing a harmless boy so it hardly seemed necessary to alarm him. I told him only that I had been shipwrecked (which was true) and that I was desperate to get back to the mainland (also true). In return for my friendship, he offered to take me with him when his father returned in forty days.

With only each other for company,

we talked a great deal and became good friends. The month passed quickly and pleasantly.

On the morning of the fortieth day, however, we were eager to be on our way and the boy was excited about life without the constant fear of death hanging over it.

'My father will be here soon,' he said. 'I must bathe and change. Will you help me?'

'Of course, I will,' I smiled.

Together we prepared the water for his bath, which took twice as long as it should have because I kept playfully throwing the water at him. Soon the ground was slippery and we were breathless with laughter. Finally, I left him alone and went to prepare some melon to eat. After a long time, when he still had not finished, I went to find him. He had slipped on the wet floor and hit his head. I had killed him without even meaning to.

I knelt beside his body and wept, but I could not risk being found there by his father. For the first time in forty days, I left the underground chamber, which now felt like a tomb. Outside, I could already see a ship on the horizon, and once again I hid from those onboard. From the cover of trees, I watched them find the trapdoor. I heard the devastated scream of the father. I cringed when the body was brought out and buried.

The ship that I had hoped to be on with my friend sailed off without me. I was alone again. For weeks I walked all over the island looking for an escape, while the sun beat down on my head. One day I was standing at the western edge when it seemed that my island prison was bigger than before, and that I was no longer so far from the mainland. By the end of a month, I was sure of it. The water in that direction was drying up to reveal cracked mud and sand. There was now only a tiny stream for me to cross.

On the other side I spied what looked like a fire in the distance, but as I drew near it turned out to be a gleaming red copper castle. It was the most wonderful building I had ever seen. As I gazed at it, an old man and ten young ones walked by, all of them handsome, all of them missing their left eye. Between the castle and the men, it was hard to tell which was the more unusual sight.

'Greetings!' they said warmly. 'You look as if you have travelled a long way. What brings you here?'

When I had finished my long story, the young men begged me to return with them to the castle. Inside it was a hall with ten blue couches serving as beds and chairs, which seemed to belong to each of the ten young men. In the middle of them

was another smaller one for the old man. With nowhere else for me to sit, I was told to sit on a carpet and to ask no questions about them or why they were all one-eyed.

When I had eaten heartily and was thinking of sleep, I overhead one young man say to the old one, 'Sheikh, it is time.'

At these words the old man rose and fetched ten basins and ten candles. He set these before the ten young men. When the blue covers were taken off the basins, I saw that they were filled with ashes, soot and coal dust. The young men mixed these all together and smeared them over their heads and faces until they were black. All the while they cried, 'This is the punishment for our faithlessness and curiosity!'

They did this for nearly the whole night. Afterwards they washed themselves carefully, put on fresh clothes and lay down to sleep. Only now I was wide awake, and curious.

I managed to bite my tongue until the next day when they took me with them on their walk. 'I am sorry to go against your wishes,' I said, 'but I must ask: why do you paint your faces? And how it is that you have all lost an eye?'

'Mind your own business,' they told me.

For the rest of that day we spoke of other things, but when night came, and the same ceremony was repeated, I begged them again to tell me the reason for it all.

'It is for your own sake,' replied one of the young men, 'that we do not tell you. If we tell you then you will share in our fate. Is that what you want?'

'Whatever the risk, I must know the answer.'

'Even though you cannot stay with us once you have lost your eye?

Our number is complete at ten, you see. We do not need an eleventh.'

'I understand,' I said, 'and I will be sad to leave you, but still I choose to know the answer to my questions.'

The matter was settled. My hosts then gave me a sheepskin, which they planned to sew me into and leave me.

'A giant bird called a roc will appear,' they explained. 'The roc will snatch you up in its talons, thinking that you are a sheep, and carry you off into the air. Do not be afraid, for he will set you down safely on a mountaintop. Then you must cut your way out of the sheepskin with this knife. Seeing that you are human, the roc will fly away.'

Here another young man took over the instructions. 'You must walk until you come to a castle covered with gold and studded with jewels. You will find the gate open. There you will learn what cost each of us our left eye and led to our nightly ritual.'

I was sewn into the sheepskin and left outside while the young men returned to the hall. The roc appeared and bore me off to its mountain nest. It was so startled when I burst from the sheepskin that it flew away.

I found the golden castle, which was even more glorious than the red copper one. The open gate led to a square court, into which opened forty doors: thirty-nine made of wood and the fortieth of solid gold. The first door was open and contained a vast hall where forty young ladies, magnificently dressed and beautiful as the moon, were seated on silk cushions.

They welcomed me with scented water to wash my hands, splendid clothes to wear and the most delicious food to eat. Afterwards they crowded close and begged me to hear of my adventures. By the time I had finished telling them, darkness had fallen. The ladies lit candles, then we sat down to a supper of dried fruits and sweetmeats, after which some ladies sang and others danced. It was delightful.

At midnight one of the ladies took me to a handsome room and left me there to sleep. For days I continued in this paradise, until one morning

I found my hosts weeping.

'What is wrong?' I asked.

'Prince,' replied one, 'we must leave you. It is unlikely we will ever meet again, unless ...'

'Unless what?' I cried.

'Unless you do as we ask.'

'Then I will,' I vowed.

'You see, we are the daughters of sultans. We live here together as you have seen, but every year we must leave for forty days for reasons we cannot tell you. Before we go, we will give you our keys so that you can explore the other doors and entertain yourself. Only the golden door must stay closed if you ever want to see us again.'

This seemed like an easy promise to make them, for I could think of nothing worse than saying goodbye to these angels forever. I was sad enough to be parted from them for forty days!

I opened a new door each day, and in this way I managed not to be bored. Sometimes I found an orchard, whose fruit was bigger than any that grew in my father's garden. Sometimes it was a courtyard planted with roses, jasmine, daffodils, tulips and lilies, and a thousand other flowers I did not know the names of. Or it was a birdhouse inhabited by all kinds of singing birds. Or a treasury heaped up with jewels of

every description. Whatever I found, it was perfection.

Thirty-nine days passed quickly, but by the fortieth I had run out of doors to explore. Then time crawled by. Finally, it occurred to me that even if I unlocked the golden door, I did not have to go inside. I could simply look from the threshold and see what wonders it contained. And I did not even have to open it fully – the barest crack would be enough for me to see through …

Arguing against my gut feeling, I turned the key. The smell that

treasury
A place where money and other valuable things are kept.

rushed to greet me was pleasant, but so strong that it made me faint. If this was a warning, I did not listen. In fact, I was all the more fascinated when I came to, and the door was now fully open. I stepped through it.

The room was large with a vaulted ceiling and scented candles in golden candlesticks. Gold and silver scented lamps hung from the ceiling too, but I paid them little attention. My eyes were on the great black horse in the corner, the handsomest I had ever seen. It was not real, of course, despite the golden troughs of barley, sesame and rose water nearby.

No, the horse was made of ebony and ivory, with a mane and tail like black thread from a fine tapestry. His saddle and bridle were made entirely of gold.

I could not resist. I mounted the creature. Had I not been alone, I would have feared looking so foolish. As it was, I went so far as to shake the red reins and flick the whip. In an instant, the ebony horse was flesh and blood and *winged*. He had wings!

Through the open door he galloped and into the open air he

ivory
A hard, off-white material that forms the tusks and teeth of elephants and other animals.

flew. All I could do was hold on as he soared higher and higher. Then, when he eventually landed, he bucked me off and kicked so wildly that I lost my left eye.

Half-stunned as I was with all that had happened, it took a moment for me to realise that I was back at the red copper castle where I had met the ten young men. I looked for them in the same hall with the ten blue couches.

They were not surprised to see me.

'All that has happened to you,' they said, 'has happened to each of us. We all enjoyed the same happiness you did, until we opened the golden door that the princesses told us not to. Now, rather than join us in our punishment, you must leave as we told you. Go to Baghdad. There you will meet the man who will decide your destiny.'

On the road to Baghdad, I shaved my head and face and put on the qalandar's clothing. Now I am here and the rest you know.

'That, madam, is my story,' the third qalandar concluded, 'and my reason for being here.'

Zobeida nodded. 'I am satisfied that all the qalandars have told the truth and suffered greatly. You are forgiven for breaking your word to ask questions. You may go.'

But still none of the qalandars left. 'I think we would all like to hear the merchants' stories,' said the third.

Zobeida turned to the caliph, the grand-vizier and the chief of the guards. 'It is your turn to speak,' she commanded

Jamal spoke for them, as usual, before the caliph could object to being ordered around. 'Madam, I can only repeat what I have said before: we are merchants come to Baghdad to sell our goods. We were shut out of our inn this evening and chanced upon your most welcoming home. We thank you for giving us shelter and we apologise for breaking our word to mind our business.'

At the end he bowed his head low, followed by the guard Mesrur and, more slowly, by the caliph.

Zobeida looked down at their bowed heads. She did not believe them. She had seen how the two older men seemed to follow and obey the younger one. 'Very well,' she said. 'If that is all then I will pardon you also, but you must leave immediately.'

Jamal breathed a sigh of relief and began to stand. The caliph held him back.

'But we haven't heard *your* story,' he pointed out.

'*My* story?' said Zobeida.

'Yes,' said the caliph. 'Why did you beat those dogs if you love them? Why is your sister covered in scars?'

'And why are you still asking questions after all I have said?' returned Zobeida.

'Because I am your caliph, Harun al-Rashid, and I demand to know!'

While Jamal and Mesrur groaned, everyone else gasped – except for

Zobeida who was not surprised to learn the merchant's true identity.

'First you break the one rule of the house that welcomed you,' she said, 'and now you order me to speak and relive a painful past. Is there no end to your rudeness?'

Harun blinked. He had not thought of it like that.

'It is only,' he began, 'because I want to help you – as I want to help the qalandars – that I *ask* you to speak …' He looked to Jamal who cocked his head pointedly. 'Please?' added Harun.

Zobeida sighed. 'You cannot help me. But I will tell you my story …'

Chapter 6
The Story of Zobeida

The two black dogs are my older sisters, Zara and Mizan. We had the same mother and father. Amina and Safie are my younger sisters, but we had different mothers. On our father's death, his wealth was divided equally among us five daughters. Then Amina and Safie went to live with their mother, and Zara, Mizan and I went to live with ours.

When our mother died, she left
us a thousand dinars each. We were
now rich enough to attract husbands,
so Zara and Mizan were soon
married. Once their money became
their husbands', it was soon spent.
I did not marry. When my sisters
left their husbands some years later,
I was able to take them into my
home and share my own money with
them, which I had saved and grown
considerably by starting a business.

After another year, and against
my advice, my sisters remarried.
Once again, they returned penniless
and heartbroken and I forgave them

for being romantic fools. We lived together as before while I continued to grow my business. Another year later I bought a merchant ship, loaded it with goods to sell and set sail with my sisters. We were headed for Basra in Iraq, but a foul wind

blew us off course to an island that even our captain had never seen.

At the base of a high mountain was a large town. While my sisters dressed, I went ashore alone. At first I was alarmed by the number of guards at the town gate, but they turned out to be made of stone. In the town itself there were similar statues, showing men, women and children in the middle of everyday activities. And in the market, too. I could find no merchants to trade with who were not also made of stone.

In the heart of the city was a palace, but all inside it were petrified.

Including the sultan and sultana. Yet from the burning torches I was sure there must be someone of flesh and blood there too. Who else could have lit them?

I soon lost track of time – and place – exploring. When I realised that I was late getting back to my sisters, I could no longer remember the way out of the palace. I was forced to rest for the night in a room that held a throne of gold and emerald, and a diamond the size of an ostrich egg. I was grateful that there were no statues there to frighten me, but it was still a restless night.

---

petrified
When living things, such as animals, plants and wood, have changed to stone.

Around midnight I heard a sound. I grabbed a torch, 'Who's there?' I demanded, running after it. From one room to the next I went, until I found one with a little carpet laid in the middle and a flesh and blood man knelt upon it in prayer. A copy of the Quran was at his side. 'Praise be to Allah!' I gasped. 'How is it that

you have not been turned to stone like the others?'

The man lifted his head to reveal a face more handsome than any I had seen. When he spoke, his voice was just as lovely and for the first time in my life, my heart skipped a beat. He looked at me like I too was a wonderful sight.

'I was not here when it happened,' he told me. 'I returned from a holy pilgrimage to find them this way. My father, the sultan, and his people were fire worshippers. I can only suppose that this was a punishment

pilgrimage
A journey to a special place for a special reason, often religious.

from God, and that you are here to save me from my loneliness.'

'Come with me,' I offered. 'I have a ship that will take you to Baghdad. There is a mighty caliph there who can help you.'

I took him back to the ship. My sisters, who had been troubled by my absence, were equally alarmed that I had returned with a man – one who made me blush whenever he was near.

We loaded the ship with as much gold, jewels and money as we could, though to take it all would have sunk us. Then we set sail again.

If I had not fallen in love with him

at first sight, I would have fallen for the prince during our voyage. The more time we spent together the closer we became – and the more jealous my sisters grew.

'Why did you bring him with you?' they demanded. 'You always said that love was foolish and men were not to be trusted.'

But it was my sisters who were not to be trusted, for they schemed behind my back.

'What if she marries him?' said Zara.

'Then all she has will be his and we will be homeless!' said Mizan. 'Again!'

Eventually, when all four of us were

together, my sisters wondered aloud, 'What will happen to our handsome prince when we reach Baghdad?'

'I will ask to marry him,' I smiled.

'And I will accept,' he smiled back.

It was what my sisters had dreaded hearing. The love they felt for me turned to anger that I would betray them for a man. That evening they threw the prince overboard. What they did not know was that he and I had arranged to meet. I saw what they did and I jumped in after him. They knew as well as I did that he could not swim. Before I could reach him, he had drowned.

The sea carried me to an island.
I forced myself to dry my clothes and
find food and water. Then I rested
in the shade of a palm tree. I was
shocked and exhausted, so at first
I thought I was seeing things. Then
I realised that what I had taken to be
a shadow was in fact a snake with a
body as thick as a tree trunk – and it
was moving towards me.

I scrambled backwards before
I understood that the snake was
not chasing me but running from
something else. There was a dragon
at its tail, which was already bloody
from having been bitten.

I felt like I was that poor snake with the wounded tail, and the dragon was my wretched sisters. I was suddenly so angry that I grabbed the nearest large stone and threw it with all of my strength. The dragon was killed instantly and the snake slithered off. As I looked at what

I had done, the tears finally came.
I wept and wept and finally slept.

In my dreams I relived all that had happened. When I awoke there was a woman standing over me with strange markings on her skin and eyes with narrow pupils.

'Who are you?' I rasped.

'I am Shahmaran,' the woman replied grandly. 'Perhaps you have heard of me?'

I replied that I had not, which seemed to annoy her. Her tongue, thin and forked, darted out.

'I am half woman, half snake and *very* powerful,' she said.

'Oh.'

'You saved my life,' Shahmaran continued, 'so I looked into your dreams to see how to repay you. I have sent a storm to sink the ship that carries your sisters. They will be drowned the same way they drowned your prince.'

'No!' I gasped.

'Why not?'

It was hard to explain. In that moment I believe I still hated my sisters, but I no longer had any wish to harm them. I knew that it would not make me feel better. It would not bring back my prince.

Shahmaran mistook my silence.

'You are right,' she said. 'Death is too quick. Come.'

Just like that, I was in my house in Baghdad. So was Shahmaran and all the palace riches that had previously been onboard the ship – plus two black dogs.

'These are your sisters,' said Shahmaran, handing me their chains. 'For betraying you and killing the prince, they will live their lives as dogs, and you will beat them every night. And though with time you may decide to forgive them and stop, you cannot. For if you do, you will be transformed as they have been.'

At the end of her story, Zobeida's eyes were wet with tears, and her sister's arms were already around her.

'That, gentlemen, is why I beat those dogs,' she said, 'and it is why I cry as I do it. I will leave it to my sister to explain her scars herself.'

At this Amina nodded, took a deep breath and began her own story …

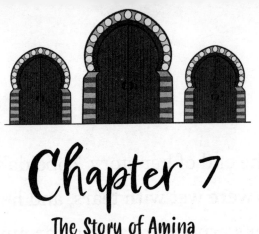

Chapter 7
The Story of Amina

As Zobeida has already said, she and I had the same father. After our father's death, I married one of the richest men in this city. After only a year of marriage my husband died and made me a very wealthy widow.

For months I stayed home in mourning, seeing no one and going nowhere. Then a woman I did not know came to see me.

'Dear lady,' she said, 'I am new to this city but I have heard much about you and it has made me bold enough to ask this. My daughter is to be married tonight but there is no one to invite who knows who we are. If you were to attend the wedding, however, others are sure to follow.'

My own loneliness moved me to accept the invitation. Before she returned to collect me, I had dressed in my favourite new dress and put on my finest jewels.

---

widow
A woman whose husband has died.
mourning
The feeling and expression of great sadness that follows a death or loss.

She took me to a magnificent house, where, rather than a wedding party, I saw only one young man.

'Where are the other guests?' I asked. 'Has no one come after all?'

The woman bowed low. 'I am sorry for tricking you, lady, but there is no wedding – although I hope there will be soon. I am this young man's housekeeper. He has long wished to meet you.'

At first I was angry, but as the young man came and spoke to me, I found him to be so charming that I forgave them both. After a few more meetings, I was in love.

One day he said, 'Will you marry me?' And I agreed. 'All I ask,' he added, 'is that you do not look at or speak to any other man but me.' Since my father was already gone and there was no other man I wished to see or speak to anyway, I agreed to this as well.

We married in private, with neither of our families present – he told me that I was all the family he

needed. One month later, I went to the market with the housekeeper and a female servant. I wished to buy my husband a present.

A merchant showed me all the best goods at his stall. 'How about this one? Or this? Feel this silk. See this quality. Isn't it beautiful? Which would you like?'

I was not allowed to look at or speak to him, so the housekeeper did everything for me. I used my finger to point out a beautiful blue dishdasha with starlight embroidery on the collar and front. I signalled

---

dishdasha
A long robe with long sleeves worn by men from Arabia.

for the housekeeper to ask the price.

The merchant answered, 'No amount of gold or money is enough for this item. But a single kiss from the young lady and it will be hers.'

My eyes flew up to the merchant's sly face. 'How rude!' I gasped, before I realised what I was doing.

'I see the price is too high for you,' said the merchant, beginning to put the long blue tunic away.

I looked down quickly, determined that I would not look or speak more than I already had. I knew that I should not, but the more I gazed at that beautiful dishdasha, the more

I thought how perfect it would look on my husband. Silently I lifted my veil so that the merchant could place a kiss on my cheek. As he walked closer, he tripped over one of the many goods he had shown me. He did kiss my cheek, but with such a force that it bruised.

That night the housekeeper applied a healing ointment to my cheek and I asked the servants to light fewer candles in the hope that my husband would not notice the bruise. At first it worked. But after I had given him the dishdasha, he wanted to see it more clearly. More candles were lit.

'What is this?' he asked, immediately concerned. 'What has happened to your face?'

What could I say? After breaking my word twice, I could not also lie to him. Nor could I bring myself to say that another man had kissed my cheek. In the end I stood there silently while his concern turned to anger and suspicion. He summoned the housekeeper.

'Now,' he demanded, 'tell me what happened to my wife's face.'

In tears she told him everything. My husband flew into a rage.

'The fact that you kept this from

me must mean that you care for this merchant!'

'No!' I gasped.

'How can I believe someone who breaks their word as you have? You will be given ten lashes for looking at, ten lashes for speaking to and thirty lashes for *kissing* another man! May the scars remind you never to break your promises, but I shall never see you again!'

He left the room and summoned a female servant – the same one who had come with me to the market and who had worked for me since my first marriage. In her hand was the whip meant to deliver my punishment, but she did not use it.

'What happened was not your fault,' she insisted. 'I will help you to escape.'

'Take this,' I said, giving her my jewelled hairpin. 'Sell it and use the money to leave this house, or you will be punished in my place.'

Her eyes were wide she took the hairpin. It was valuable enough to change her life. 'I will, lady. Thank you.'

'Thank *you*,' I said fiercely.

Together we tied bedsheets together and I escaped out of the window. I was almost at the bottom when I realise that my makeshift rope was not quite long enough. I was forced to jump the rest of the

way. I landed in a rose bush whose thorns cut me as surely as the whip would have. Then I fled to my sister Zobeida's house, where I have lived ever since.

Amina stopped talking and took her sister's hand, squeezing it gratefully.

'That, gentlemen, is why I am covered in scars,' she concluded.

The caliph was outraged.

'No husband of honour would threaten his wife so! What is his name?'

But a strange look passed between Amina and Zobeida that convinced him they would not tell him willingly. Fortunately, he had another way to find out.

'Thank you for sharing your stories,' he said. 'I see now why you did not want to relive such painful memories. Now that you have, I hope that I can help.' He turned to Zobeida. 'Madam, do you know the name of the island you washed up on, or where else to find the snake lady who transformed your sisters into dogs?'

'I do not,' answered Zobeida, 'but she said that one day I would need her, and on that day I should burn two of her hairs to summon her.'

'And you have those hairs?'

Zobeida pulled a curious pendant from her dress that opened to reveal two black hairs. 'I carry them with me everywhere.'

'I knew you would,' the caliph said admiringly. 'Please burn them now.'

Zobeida's first instinct was to say no. She had no wish to see the snake woman again, or to risk herself or her half-sisters becoming dogs as well. But something about the way the caliph was looking at her, with

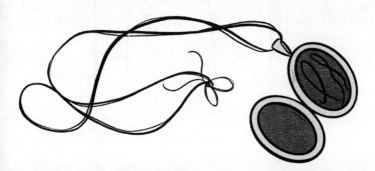

calm, confident – and yes, *beautiful* – eyes made her agree.

The hairs burnt up in one flash and Shahmaran appeared the next. She was facing the caliph.

The snake woman was startled. 'Who are you?'

'I am Caliph Harun al-Rashid ibn Muḥammad al-Mahdi ibn al-Manṣur al-'Abbasi, Commander of the Faithful. Perhaps you have heard of me?'

The snake woman blinked several times. Then she eyed his merchant clothing. 'You do not look like a caliph.'

'Nevertheless, I am *very* powerful.'

'What do you want from me?'

'First I want you to restore the dog sisters to their former bodies.'

'Why would I do that?'

'Because I am a collector of stories and you want your name and power to be known. Do as I say and your name will live forever in my library – the greatest library of the greatest caliph there has ever been.'

The snake woman folded her arms. 'You said "first". What is the second thing you want?'

'I want you to heal Amina's scars and tell me the name of her unworthy husband.'

Amina and Zobeida exchanged another look. Shahmaran smirked. 'Very well. Bring forth Amina, the dogs and a glass of water.'

The snake woman said some words over the water. When she cast it over the dogs, they were transformed back into Zara and Mizan. When she did the same to Amina, her scars disappeared.

'Now for the answer to your question,' grinned Shahmaran, revealing sharp white fangs. 'Amina's husband is none other than your eldest son, Prince Abad.'

If the snake woman had hoped to shock the caliph into behaving badly, she was disappointed. Certainly, he was shocked, but he behaved in such a way that Zobeida in particular was impressed. He thanked the snake woman, who left with a final flick of her tongue. Then he sent Mesrur to bring his son.

While they waited, the caliph and Zobeida talked and discovered much in common. Then Prince Abad arrived, took one look at Amina and turned very pale.

'I see you know this woman,' said his father. He sighed deeply. 'You were always a jealous boy, Abad but wives are not toys to be thrown away when they displease you. If Amina will still have you, I command that you take back your wife and be a better husband. As for her sister,' and here he turned to Zobeida, 'when I entered your home last night my heart was my own, this morning it is yours. You are clever and brilliant

and brave, and I am your humble servant. Marry me.'

Zobeida smiled. 'Is that a command too?'

'A plea,' he smiled back.

'Then yes.'

The two of them were married and all of Baghdad rejoiced. In the happy days that followed, Zobeida's three sisters also found love with the three qalandars, who were given new lands and palaces by the caliph.

The porter, of course, complained loudly.